Dear Parents:

Congratulations! Your child is taking the first steps on an exciting journey. The destination? Independent reading!

STEP INTO READING® will help your child get there. The program offers five steps to reading success. Each step includes fun stories and colorful art or photographs. In addition to original fiction and books with favorite characters, there are Step into Reading Non-Fiction Readers, Phonics Readers and Boxed Sets, Sticker Readers, and Comic Readers—a complete literacy program with something to interest every child.

Learning to Read, Step by Step!

Ready to Read   Preschool–Kindergarten
• big type and easy words • rhyme and rhythm • picture clues
For children who know the alphabet and are eager to begin reading.

Reading with Help   Preschool–Grade 1
• basic vocabulary • short sentences • simple stories
For children who recognize familiar words and sound out new words with help.

Reading on Your Own   Grades 1–3
• engaging characters • easy-to-follow plots • popular topics
For children who are ready to read on their own.

Reading Paragraphs   Grades 2–3
• challenging vocabulary • short paragraphs • exciting stories
For newly independent readers who read simple sentences with confidence.

Ready for Chapters   Grades 2–4
• chapters • longer paragraphs • full-color art
For children who want to take the plunge into chapter books but still like colorful pictures.

STEP INTO READING® is designed to give every child a successful reading experience. The grade levels are only guides; children will progress through the steps at their own speed, developing confidence in their reading. The F&P Text Level on the back cover serves as another tool to help you choose the right book for your child.

Remember, a lifetime love of reading starts with a single step!

To Leo, Della, Abe, and Layla,
with love —M.B.

To my littlest sis, Aubrey C.
—H.H.

Text copyright © 2020 by Maribeth Boelts
Cover art and interior illustrations copyright © 2020 by Hollie Hibbert

All rights reserved. Published in the United States by Random House Children's Books, a division of Penguin Random House LLC, New York.

Step into Reading, Random House, and the Random House colophon are registered trademarks of Penguin Random House LLC.

Visit us on the Web!
StepIntoReading.com
rhcbooks.com

Educators and librarians, for a variety of teaching tools, visit us at RHTeachersLibrarians.com

Library of Congress Cataloging-in-Publication Data
Names: Boelts, Maribeth, author. | Hibbert, Hollie, illustrator.
Title: The gingerbread pup / by Maribeth Boelts ; illustrated by Hollie Hibbert.
Description: New York : Random House Children's Books, [2020]
Series: Step into reading. Step 3 | Audience: Ages 5–8. | Audience: Grades 2–3.
Summary: Evalina dreams of having a dog to help with her troublesome sheep, but when she bakes a gingerbread dog he wreaks havoc all over town.
Identifiers: LCCN 2019034959 (print) | LCCN 2019034960 (ebook)
ISBN 978-0-525-58200-7 (trade paperback) | ISBN 978-0-525-58201-4 (library binding)
ISBN 978-0-525-58202-1 (ebook)
Subjects: CYAC: Gingerbread—Fiction. | Dogs—Fiction. | Sheep—Fiction.
Classification: LCC PZ7.B6338 Gin 2020 (print) | LCC PZ7.B6338 (ebook) | DDC [E]—dc23

Printed in the United States of America

10 9 8 7 6 5 4 3 2

This book has been officially leveled by using the F&P Text Level Gradient™ Leveling System.

The Gingerbread Pup

by Maribeth Boelts

illustrated by Hollie Hibbert

Random House 🏠 New York

Once upon a time,

there was a girl named Evalina.

Evalina lived all alone.

She tended her sheep.

But her sheep did not

want to be tended.

They jumped the fence.

They hid in the woods.

They ran through the village.

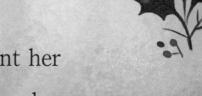

Evalina spent her
days chasing sheep.

"How I would love to have a dog!"

said Evalina.

"We could be best friends.

We could tend the sheep together."

One day, Evalina made
gingerbread cookies.
"No gingerbread boy
for me," she said.
"I will make a
gingerbread pup instead!"

Evalina cut out a gingerbread pup.

She baked it in the oven.

The yummy smell filled the house.

Evalina opened the oven
to check on
the gingerbread pup.

The gingerbread pup

sprang to life!

It popped out of the oven.

"Yip, yip, yip!" barked

the gingerbread pup.

The gingerbread pup
spun in circles.

It jumped on the furniture.

Then it raced out the door!

flour

"Stop!" called Evalina.

But the gingerbread pup

did not stop.

The gingerbread pup
found the sheep.
It chased them
right into the mud!
"Baaaaa," said the sheep.
"Oh no!" cried Evalina.

The gingerbread pup
raced through the village.
"That pup stole my hat!"

"That pup broke my eggs!"

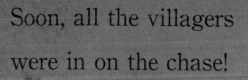

Soon, all the villagers

were in on the chase!

The gingerbread pup
came to a river.

How would it get across?

The gingerbread pup
saw a shaggy dog
by the riverbank.

"Give me a ride
across the river, dog!"
said the gingerbread pup.

The gingerbread pup climbed on
the shaggy dog's tail.
The shaggy dog
waded into the river.
He began to paddle.
The gingerbread pup
teased the crowd.
"Nah, nah, nah, nah,
boo-boo!"

"You are going to get wet,"
said the shaggy dog.

"Climb on my back."

The gingerbread pup climbed on
the shaggy dog's back.

The water grew deeper.
"Better move to my head,"
said the shaggy dog.

The gingerbread pup climbed on
the shaggy dog's head.

Then it slid down
to the tip of his nose!
"Wheee!" said the
gingerbread pup.

The shaggy dog's whiskers
twitched.

The shaggy dog's belly
growled.

He was so hungry!

Sniff, sniff, sniff!

Evalina gasped.

The villagers gasped too.

They all knew the story

of the gingerbread boy

who gets eaten by the fox.

"The gingerbread pup

is a goner!" said Evalina.

But the shaggy dog kept paddling.

He didn't play mean tricks

like the fox in the story.

"Does that shaggy dog
belong to anyone?"
asked Evalina.
A man shrugged.
"He's a stray."

The shaggy dog carried
the gingerbread pup
across the river.
He jumped onto the shore.
Evalina scooped up
the gingerbread pup.

"You're coming home with me,
Gingerbread Pup,"
said Evalina.
Then Evalina petted the shaggy dog.
"Thank you," she said.
The shaggy dog wagged his tail
and licked Evalina's hand.
Evalina looked into
his big brown eyes.
She smiled.

"Would you like to
come home with us?"
asked Evalina.
"Ruff! Ruff! Ruff!" barked
the shaggy dog.
Evalina laughed.
"I'll name you Ruffles!"
she said.

At home,

the gingerbread pup

got into every kind of trouble.

It scattered the sheep.

It yipped and yapped.

It escaped out the window.

"What can we do about
the gingerbread pup?"
said Evalina.

Ruffles brought Evalina
a cookie cutter.
"You want me to make
a gingerbread boy?"
asked Evalina.

"Ruff!" said Ruffles.
Evalina made a
gingerbread boy and
slid it into the oven.

A few minutes later,
Evalina opened the oven.
The gingerbread boy
sprang to life!

Out of the house he ran!
"Catch me if you can!"
said the gingerbread boy.
"Yip, yip, yip!" barked
the gingerbread pup,
and raced after him.

From that day on,
Evalina, Ruffles,
and the sheep
lived happily ever after.

The gingerbread pup
and the gingerbread boy
lived happily ever after too!